Gert & Frieda

Anita Riggio

ATHENEUM 1990 NEW YORK

For Alice

Gert and Frieda were friends.

In happy times, they hugged each other around their
middles, and when times turned tough, they clutched
tight and waited for the bad times to pass. This is the
way things were.

One morning, Frieda called Gert on the phone.

"Hello, Gert. This is Frieda."

"I know."

"How did you know?"

"You call me every morning. I'm used to your voice."

"Well, I'm coming over. Is that all right?"

"Certainly it's all right," Gert said. And Frieda did.

Frieda opened the door to Gert's house and walked directly to the dining table, where she placed a crinkled-up brown bag.

"Pumpkin-date bread. My famous. Very delicious,"
Frieda said. Then she draped herself across the table.

Her shoulders drooped. Her head drooped. Her hat drooped. Her plume was not perky, either.

Gert poured tea. "Thank you for the bread, Frieda. What's the problem?"

"What makes you think there's a problem?"

Gert sliced the pumpkin-date bread. "Because every time there's a problem, you bake something, and bring it over, and fling yourself across my table."

"I do?"

"Certainly." Gert sipped her tea. "So what's the problem?"

"I'm bored!" Frieda wailed. "Bored. Bored! *Bored*!"

"Really," Gert said. "With what?"

"With everything!" Frieda moaned.

"I'm *bored* with my same old boots.

I'm *bored* with my same old hat.

I'm *bored* with my same old pumpkin-date bread!"

"Very delicious." Gert nibbled the bread.

"Thank you," Frieda heaved. "I'm still not happy."

"I can see that," Gert said. She moved Frieda's arm and sat down.

"Then change a little something. Buy new red boots."

"I just bought these."

"Add a bit more nutmeg to your pumpkin-date."

"It's perfect the way it is."

"Okay. Then take your hat off."

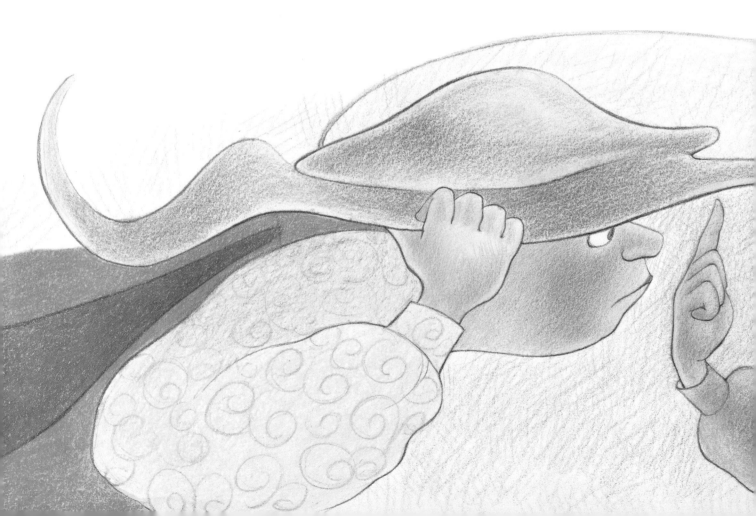

"I can't," Frieda gasped. "I never take my hat off."

"I know," Gert replied. "But you may find it easier to hold your head up without that hat....You'll feel different."

"How different?"

"Different. Take the hat off for a while. You'll see."

Frieda stood up, gingerly lifted the hat from her head, and laid it on the table.

"There," Frieda grumped. She patted the plume anxiously.

"There," said Gert. "So how does it feel?"

"Different. It's lighter out here."

"Yes, it is."

"It's much cooler out here, too."

"Oh, much."

The next day, Frieda called Gert. "Hello, Gert. This is Frieda. May I come right over?"

"Certainly," Gert replied.

When she hung up, Gert arranged the tea cups on the table. She filled the kettle with water and set it on the stove to boil. She fiddled with a saucer. She frowned at the kettle. "I'll just sit and wait," Gert decided.

They strolled through a pine grove. The needles brushed their heads as they passed under the boughs.

"Scratchy," Frieda muttered. She selected seven dainty pine cones. Those went into her hat, too.

"Look there, Gert!" Frieda whooped. "It's an abandoned nest! Hold my hat!" Frieda shinnied up the tree to retrieve the nest.

"That's enough," she said, when she climbed back down. "Let's go home."

Gert looked puzzled.

Outside the squirrels chattered.
"What a racket," Frieda
grumbled. She picked three long
green shoots with fuzzy flowers on
the ends and put them in her hat.

"I'm hot," Frieda whined, as she
gathered four shiny green leaves. She
put those in her hat.

"What are you doing, Frieda?"
Gert asked.
"Rummaging," Frieda sighed.

"What are you rummaging for?"
Gert wanted to know.
"Treasures," Frieda replied.

"I feel light-headed."

"I imagine you do."

"I think I'm going to faint."
Frieda swooned.

"I doubt that," Gert said.
"Let's go for a walk."

Frieda blanched. "I need to bring
my hat."

"Naturally," said Gert.

A moment later, there came a knock at the door. "Come in, Frieda," Gert called. The door did not open. "Come in, Frieda!" Gert sang out. Still no Frieda.

Gert walked briskly to the door and swung it open. "Frieda?"

A lopsided stack of hats shuffled through the door.

"Look, Gert," Frieda chirped. "Remember the three long shoots, the four shiny leaves, the seven dainty pine cones, and the nest?"

"Yes," Gert said. "I remember."

"Well, I made *this* hat from *those* treasures!"

"Oh, my!" breathed Gert.

"Then I did *more* rummaging and found *more* treasures to make *more* hats."

"You made this one from your butterfly net!" Gert squealed.

"It had a hole in it, anyway!" Frieda sang.

"You made this one from the *Daily Scoop*!" Gert hooted.

"It has a recipe for cranberry-nut bread!" Frieda hummed.

"Look! I made this one from my fruit bowl
and the fruit!"

"The fruit bowl *and* the fruit?"

"Yes!" Frieda panted. "The fruit was squishy, anyhow!"

"But I made the *best* hat of all for you, Gert . . .

my most treasured friend.''

"Thank you," Gert giggled.
"Thank *you*," Frieda beamed.

And they hugged each other around their middles.

Frieda's Famous

very delicious!

PUMPKIN DATE BREAD

This recipe makes two loaves—one for you and one for a friend!

What You'll Need:

2 cups brown sugar
½ cup oil
¼ cup molasses
2 cups pumpkin
3 eggs
3 cups flour

1 teaspoon baking soda
1 teaspoon baking powder
1 teaspoon salt
1 teaspoon cinnamon
½ teaspoon cloves
½ teaspoon mace

½ teaspoon nutmeg
2 cups chopped dates
large and small mixing bowls
spoon
two small loaf pans
(4½″ x 8½″ x 2½″)

What to Do:

1. Preheat oven to 350 degrees Fahrenheit.
2. In the large bowl, mix sugar, oil, and molasses. Blend well.
3. Add pumpkin and eggs. Stir.
4. In a small bowl, mix flour, baking soda, baking powder, salt, cinnamon, cloves, mace, and nutmeg.
5. Add these dry ingredients to the pumpkin mixture. Blend well.
6. Stir in dates.
7. Pour the batter into the ungreased loaf pans. Be sure to divide the batter evenly.
8. Bake for one hour and fifteen minutes, or until a toothpick inserted in the center of the breads comes out clean.
9. Using oven mitts, carefully remove the breads from the oven and let them cool slightly in the pans.
10. Remove the loaves from the pans and place them on a wire rack until the breads are just warm to the touch.
11. Cut in thick slices and serve with tea to your best friend!

★ *(Frieda suggests that you ask an adult to help.)* ★

Atheneum
Macmillan Publishing Company
866 Third Avenue, New York, NY 10022
Collier Macmillan Canada, Inc.
First Edition
Printed in USA

Library of Congress Cataloging-in-Publication Data
Riggio, Anita.
Gert and Frieda / written and illustrated by Anita Riggio.
—1st ed.   p.   cm.
Summary: As a cure for her boredom, Frieda suggests that Gert
change her hat.
ISBN 0-689-31568-6
[1. Boredom—Fiction.   2. Hats—Fiction.   3. Friendship—Fiction.]
I. Title.
PZ7.R44187Ge   1990
[E]—dc20
89-32356   CIP   AC

WITH THANKS TO JON LANMAN